Homecoming: Shafer's Tale of Lost and Found

Published by Theresa D. Tillinger, Franklin TN 37064

Printed in the United States of America

First Printing, 2018

ISBN 978-0-692-93617-7

Shatoi and Harper
Thank you for supporting
pet charities!

Homecoming

Shafer's Tale of Lost & Found

By: Patti B. Freeman & Theresa D. Tillinger

Illustrated By: Jason S. Brock

My name is Shafer! Delighted to meet you! Tell you a story? Don't mind if I do!

I lived far away with my mom and dad,
but we were back home and we were very glad

We gave our new place a wonderful name -
"HOMECOMING it is!", my dad did proclaim.

I have many friends who live here with me,
I'll show you around - they're all nice. You'll see.

There's Luna and Tuna, cats chasing the mice.
Most of the time they are very nice.

Out in the coop are Minnie and Pennie.
I love their eggs - they always lay plenty.

While on my walks I talk to Sherlock.
He's high in the sky because he's a hawk.

Often I wave to Shamir the Deer.
He wanders the fields and the woods without fear.

I see Myrtle D. Turtle enjoying a swim
I love to join her -
It helps me stay trim.

The end of the day ends my wonderful roam.
I get very tired and head for my home.

I say goodnight to Howell the Owl.
I go to sleep while he's on the prowl.

One morning I wanted to go for a snoop,
for I discovered that all my friends POOP!

"YUCK!", said my mom. My feast was now crushed
"My oh my Shafer! Your teeth must be brushed."

But I like smelly things, so I swam in the pond,
with Myrtle D. Turtle - we have such a bond.

"Oh no!", said my dad as he ran down the path.
"Now we will have to give you a bath!"

"At least you"ll be clean and not such a sight
when we go for a ride in the car late tonight."

Yippee! Yipee! I love a joyride,
Smelling the smells of the nice countryside.

My head's out the window, and so was my paw.
Uh oh! I tumbled - it was quite a fall!

I was not hurt, but where was my car?
It went down the road and seemed very far.

What would I do all alone and afraid?
I needed some help so I prayed and I prayed.

Howell the Owl answered my prayer.
"I'm here for you. Do not despair."

"I'm here for you too!", said Shamir the Deer.
"Sleep in soft leaves and dry those tears."

I woke the next morning, thirsty and hungry.
And truth be told, I felt a bit grungy.

I followed my friends and we went for a walk,
when suddenly appeared Sherlock the Hawk.

"I can see all from high in the sky.
To the fields and the streams we will go, you and I."

You'll find plenty to eat - there's poop all around.
In the streams and ponds much water abounds."

I was enjoying my time with my friends,
exploring the hills and sniffing the wind.

But then I was sad - I had to get home,
I missed mom and dad so we went for a roam.

We wandered and wandered to the edge of a cliff.
From there we saw far and I could sniff.

We saw many cars along curvy roads,
and people with signs - there were loads and loads!

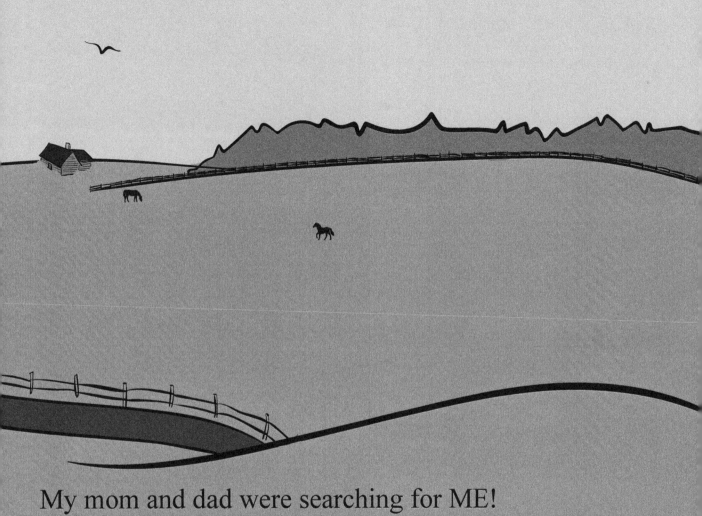

My mom and dad were searching for ME!
I told my friends, "We'll find them, you'll see."

Off we went through the woods, past rivers and streams,
forever and ever, and ever it seemed.

We came to a hillside and stopped to see.
They were, we could tell, still looking for me.

Now they had help - a dog and Miss Daisy.
That dog was so small - I thought they were crazy!

I heard them say the dog's name was Harper,
and boy oh boy, she was a barker!

Miss Daisy gave Harper my fur to sniff.
She knew where to look from that little whiff!

Harper took off towards the woods very fast,
in hopes that this searching would end at last.

All followed Harper calling my name,
but they had to stop when darkness came.

While they were searching, we too were busy.
We were excited and all in a tizzy!

My friends and I ran fast toward the sounds,
but got very tired and had to slow down.

We walked a bit longer, then laid down to rest.
I dreamt of my family, got sad and depressed.

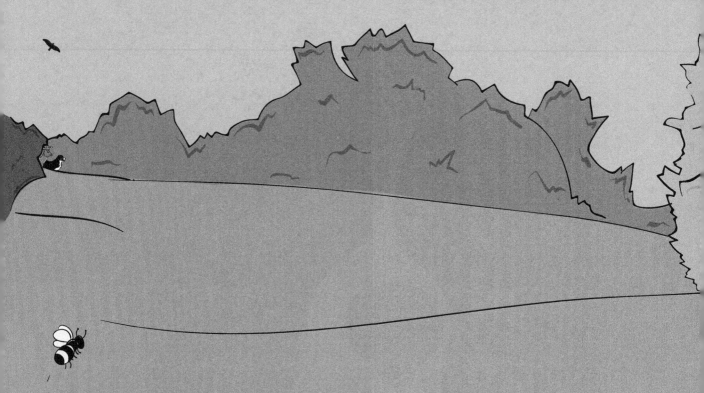

A new day began with my friends on our search,
with Sherlock the Hawk as a guide from his perch.

My mom and my dad began their search too,
on a beautiful morning, the ground wet with dew.

"Today is the day!", I said to my friends.
I really did hope our search would soon end.

As we were walking I heard
a new sound.

It was sniffing and
scratching and close
to the ground.

I ran towards the sound as fast as I could.
They were calling my name - this had to be good.

Harper was leading Miss Daisy and dad.
Mom was there too - they were no longer sad.

Sherlock the Hawk let out a squawk
and said to keep running just past the rock.

I did as he said with great leaps and bounds.
Then suddenly saw them. Oh joy- I was found

We hugged and we kissed and rolled on the ground,
with laughing and barking, and love all around.

My old friends were there when I returned home,
and they were so glad I'd returned from my roam.

Luna and Tuna, the cats, lowdly purred.
Which Minnie and Pennie thought quite absurd!

Shamir the Deer smiled from beyond,
while Myrtle D. Turtle splashed in the pond.

Get back to normal - that seemed the plan.
Until I found out - Harper's in the clan!

"Harper's retiring - she's done with her work",
said Sherlock the Hawk with a bit of a smirk.

"She needs a new home and it seems only right,
to be here with you beginning tonight."

"That's great with me!", I said so excited.
I really and truly was quite delighted.

Later that night, as I was dreaming,
I saw that the name of our house had new meaning.

All of my friends had helped me get home.
They made me feel safe and loved on my roam.

My heart and my family are now overflowing.
Homecoming is where there is love ever growing.

Harper's
Hidden Critter
Challenge

Be a detective just like Harper!

Harper used her amazing senses to find Shafer. Now she is challenging you to find the critters hidden thoughout this book. Look carefully because you just might miss them. Harper has listed below the critters you must find...good luck!

3 Ladybugs   2 Field Mice   1 Earthworm

2 Raccoons   1 Fly   2 Snails

3 Bees

5 Lightning Bugs   1 Fish

2 Dragonflies

14 Ants   3 Butterflies   2 Grasshoppers

CPSIA information can be obtained
at www.ICGtesting.com
Printed in the USA
LVOW05*1555050318
568695LV00006B/45/P